P9-DNQ-485

How to use this book

Read the captions, then turn to the sticker pages
and choose the picture that best fits in the space available.
(Hint: check the sticker labels for helpful clues!)

•

Don't forget that your stickers can be stuck down and peeled off again.
If you are careful, you can even use your stickers more than once.

There are lots of fantastic extra stickers too!

LONDON, NEW YORK, MUNICH,
MELBOURNE, AND DELHI

Written and edited by Helen Murray
Designed by Lisa Robb
Styling and Jacket designed by Lisa Lanzarini

First American Edition, 2012
10 9 8 7 6 5 4 3
011—183100—Mar/2012

Published in the United States by
DK Publishing
345 Hudson Street
New York, New York 10014

ISBN: 978-0-7566-9049-6

Color reproduction by MDP, UK
Printed and bound by L-Rex Printing Co., Ltd, China

Discover more at
www.dk.com
www.LEGO.com
www.starwars.com

Timeline

Republic Era

The LEGO *Star Wars* galaxy is a peaceful
Republic, led by the elected Senate and
the secretive Chancellor Palpatine.

The Clone Wars

A group called the Separatists attack
the Republic. They are led by Count
Dooku, but they are secretly controlled
by a Sith Lord named Darth Sidious.
The Republic forms an army of clone
troopers, led by Jedi generals, to defend
the galaxy against the Separatist
Droid Army.

Empire Era

Darth Sidious takes over the LEGO *Star
Wars* galaxy and makes himself the
Emperor. The Rebel Alliance (or Rebels)
come together to fight against the
Empire and restore peace to the galaxy.

Jedi Knights

The Jedi are the guardians of peace in the LEGO *Star Wars* galaxy. Jedi minifigures all carry lightsabers because sometimes they must battle to maintain peace. Jedi come from species and planets across the galaxy, so there are many different-looking minifigures. Who is your favorite?

Qui-Gon Jinn
This brave Jedi Master carries out missions in seven LEGO *Star Wars* sets. He wears a traditional Jedi tunic and cape.

Aayla Secura
Aayla is a skilled Twi'lek Jedi Knight. Her minifigure wears a helmet and has Twi'lek tentacles that hang behind her back.

Ahsoka Tano
Ahsoka is a Togruta Jedi apprentice. She has Togruta head-tails that look like hair—they are still growing because she is young.

Luminara Unduli
Luminara is a Mirialan Jedi. Can you see the tattoos on her chin? Mirialans tattoo their bodies when they achieve important new skills.

Barriss Offee

Barriss is a Jedi in training. She learns the ways of the Force from fellow Mirialan minifigure Luminara.

Nahdar Vebb

This Mon Calamari Jedi minifigure is passionate about defending the galaxy. He may be young, but he is very skilled with a lightsaber.

Quinlan Vos

Quinlan is an expert Force tracker—he can track down anybody! He has messy hair and a stubbled face—he is a scruffy minifigure!

Jedi Knight

A minifigure with no name! This mysterious Jedi is transported on a Republic gunship in one LEGO® set.

The Jedi Council

The Jedi are governed by the Jedi Council, which is made up of the wisest and most respected Jedi minifigures in the LEGO *Star Wars* galaxy. Council members are Jedi who have proved themselves to be incredibly skilled and powerful. Which Jedi Council minifigure do you think is the best?

Yoda

Yoda is one of the most powerful and respected Jedi of all time. His minifigure may be small, but size matters not.

Obi-Wan Kenobi

Brave Jedi Obi-Wan carries a blue lightsaber, but he uses it only if he is really in danger.

Shaak Ti

Shaak Ti is a Togruta Jedi from Shili. Unlike Ahsoka Tano, her minifigure has long head-tails because she is an adult.

Mace Windu

Mace Windu is the only minifigure to use a purple lightsaber. He is one of the best duelists in the galaxy!

Plo Koon

Plo Koon is a great Jedi from Dorin. He wears gray goggles and a mask to breathe on other planets.

Saesee Tiin

Saesee Tiin is one of the best pilots in history. His Iktotchi minifigure has down-turned horns.

Ki-Adi-Mundi

Ki-Adi-Mundi is a very clever Jedi from Cerea. He has a specially enlarged head mold so that his huge brain can fit inside!

Eeth Koth

Eeth Koth is a Zabrak Jedi with a strong connection to the Force. His minifigure has a horned head, tattoos, and hair tied back with rope.

Obi-Wan "Ben" Kenobi

Old Obi-Wan is in hiding, but there is no mistaking this minifigure, holding his blue lightsaber.

Anakin Skywalker

There are 15 minifigures of Anakin showing how he changes from a young slave boy on Tatooine into one of the greatest Jedi Knights ever known. Anakin's fateful transformation to the dark side is also brought to life in his minifigures. Which Anakin minifigure do you like best?

Boy Anakin
Anakin is a slave boy. He works hard and shows great promise. Look at his minifigure's short legs—they show he is still a child.

Podracer Anakin
This minifigure also has short legs. Anakin may be young, but he is already a star pilot. His expression shows that he is determined to win!

Clone Wars Anakin
Anakin is known throughout the galaxy as the "Hero With No Fear." His minifigure's face is scarred and battle-worn.

Jedi Anakin
Poor Anakin lost his arm in a deadly duel with a Sith Lord. His minifigure now wears a black glove to hide his cyborg arm.

Padawan Anakin
Headstrong Anakin is a Jedi apprentice to his mentor Obi-Wan Kenobi. Can you see the Padawan braid printed on his torso?

Parka Anakin

Somewhere beneath the hood, goggles, and bandana is Anakin Skywalker! His minifigure wears snow gear to travel to ice planets.

Sith Apprentice Anakin

Anakin's minifigure's eyes are Sith-yellow. He has turned to the dark side and is now a Sith apprentice named Darth Vader.

Battle-Damaged Anakin

Anakin carries a red Sith lightsaber, which he has already used for evil. His injured minifigure has to wear a helmet to breathe.

Meet Darth Vader

Look under Darth Vader's helmet and his scarred gray face is revealed. It is hard to believe that this Sith minifigure was ever Anakin.

The Sith

Secretive and power-hungry, the Sith lurk in the shadows of the LEGO *Star Wars* galaxy. The minifigures are evil-looking and use the dark side of the Force to take control at any cost. Who do you think is the most evil Sith minifigure?

Chancellor Palpatine
Nobody knows, but Chancellor Palpatine is actually Darth Sidious in disguise! He is the most powerful Sith Lord in history.

Emperor Palpatine
Palpatine now rules the galaxy. A big hood hides his scary eyes and face.

Hologram Palpatine
Secretive Palpatine communicates with Darth Vader by hologram.

Count Dooku
Villainous Dooku is Darth Sidious's Sith apprentice in disguise. His minifigure has a lightsaber with a curved hilt.

Darth Vader
Darth Vader strikes fear across the galaxy in 16 LEGO *Star Wars* sets. His minifigures all have the iconic black helmet piece.

Asajj Ventress
Ventress is a deadly assassin who works for Count Dooku. She wields twin red lightsabers to attack the Jedi.

Darth Maul
Sith apprentice Darth Maul uses a terrifying double-bladed lightsaber. His minifigure's face is covered in tattoos.

Savage Opress
Count Dooku's Sith apprentice is on a secret mission to destroy his own Master! He is armed with a double-bladed lightsaber and blade.

Galen Marek
This mysterious minifigure is Darth Vader's secret apprentice. He appears in just one LEGO *Star Wars* set.

Friendly Aliens

The LEGO *Star Wars* galaxy is filled with friendly and helpful aliens. These minifigures may look cute, but don't be fooled—some of them battle hard and are fiercely protective of their home planets and their friends. Which LEGO *Star Wars* alien minifigure would you like on your side?

Jar Jar Binks
Jar Jar is a very clumsy, but well-meaning Gungan from the planet Naboo. His minifigure has long ears and eyes on stalks.

Thi-Sen
Thi-Sen is Chief of the Talz on the planet Orto Plutonia. He carries a spear to protect his tribe from unfriendly visitors.

Gungan Soldier
The Gungans join forces with the Jedi to protect Naboo. This brave soldier fights off the droid army with his energy shield and stick.

Wookiee Warrior
The Wookiees' home planet of Kashyyyk is invaded by Separatists. This Wookiee warrior minifigure uses his deadly spear to defend it.

Wicket W. Warrick

Wicket is a friendly Ewok from Endor. Ewoks are small and furry—their minifigures have short, unmovable LEGO legs.

Logray

Logray is an Ewok shaman. He wears a headdress with a bird skeleton and feathers. Be careful, or he could put a curse on you!

Chief Chirpa

This wise old Ewok Chief leads his tribe into battle. His minifigure carries a staff topped with animal horns.

Onaconda Farr

Onaconda Farr is a Senator from the planet Rodia. His minifigure has green skin, a snout, and large glassy eyes.

Wald

Wald helps his friend Anakin build a Podracer. His minifigure wears a slave tunic and has short legs because he is a child.

Not-so-friendly Aliens

Beware! Although there are many friendly alien minifigures in the LEGO *Star Wars* galaxy, you may be unlucky enough to meet one of these nasty minifigures. They are greedy, corrupt, and sometimes deadly. Which LEGO *Star Wars* alien minifigure would you least like to encounter?

Tusken Raider
The Sand People are fiercely hostile to other minifigures. Wearing sand-colored shrouds, they move unnoticed across the desert.

Nute Gunray
This greedy Nemoidian secretly works with the Sith. His minifigure wears elegant robes and a headdress—and a constant frown!

Wampa
Wampas live on the ice planet Hoth. This minifigure has big teeth and claws, which she uses to attack unwelcome visitors.

Mandalorian
The Mandalorian is a deadly soldier. His minifigure's armor is known throughout the galaxy for being almost indestructible.

Jawa
Droids, beware! This industrious little minifigure spends his days scavenging for droid parts on the planet Tatooine.

Sebulba

Sebulba is a tricky Podracer and young Anakin's arch rival. This unusual minifigure walks on his arms and uses his legs to steer!

Geonosian Warrior

These bug-like minifigures live on the planet Geonosis. This nasty warrior carries a sonic blaster to attack the Jedi.

Gasgano

Fiendish Gasgano is another Podracing rival of Anakin. His minifigure's many arms allow him to race at super-fast speeds.

Clone Troopers

The LEGO *Star Wars* galaxy is at war. Led by Jedi Generals, thousands of clone trooper minifigures defend the galaxy against the Separatists' Droid Army. Although clone troopers are identical at first, many are trained for specialist missions and wear individual uniforms. Can you tell them apart?

Clone Trooper
These minifigures all wear identical white armor and helmets. They are equipped with blaster rifles to destroy the Separatists.

Captain Rex
Captain Rex is General Anakin Skywalker's second-in-command. His minifigure wears extra armor for dangerous missions.

Commander Fox
Commander Fox battles the mighty spider droid. No wonder he carries two blaster pistols and wears extra leg armor!

Commander Cody
Cody serves under Obi-Wan Kenobi. His minifigure's orange markings reflect his rank and unit.

Commander Wolffe
This tough minifigure leads the Wolf Pack. His helmet has a rangefinder that feeds into a computer screen in his visor.

Kashyyyk Trooper

You might find it hard to spot this minifigure in jungle worlds, but he'll see you! He wears green armor and a special visor.

Bomb Squad Trooper

You can spot a bomb squad trooper by his orange armor. He wears an extra-sturdy helmet to protect against blasts.

ARC Trooper

This Advanced Recon Commando is one of the most skilled soldier minifigures in the galaxy.

Commander Gree

Commander Gree's minifigure battles the Geonosians with a large blaster rifle. He has extra ammunition on his torso.

Aerial Trooper

The aerial trooper zooms into battle with rocket-powered wings and a super-sized sniper rifle.

The Droid Army

The Separatist Droid Army is the biggest minifigure army in LEGO *Star Wars* history. Led by a brutal warrior, the army relies on its huge numbers. Some droids are more advanced than others, but they all pose danger to the minifigure heroes of the Republic. Which do you think is the deadliest?

General Grievous
This vicious minifigure is Supreme Commander of the droid army. But don't call him a droid! He is a cyborg—part flesh, part metal.

Battle Droid
Standard battle droids have plain torsos. They are controlled by a central computer and make up the majority of the minifigure army.

Droid Commander
This minifigure leads his battle droid army into battle against the Republic. His yellow torso signifies his rank.

Rocket Droid Commander
Equipped with a blaster and rocket pack, this minifigure can attack enemy life pods in space.

Security Battle Droid
This droid minifigure uses his advanced programming to detect threats against the Separatists. You can spot him by his red torso.

Super Battle Droid
This hulking minifigure is bigger, stronger, and has more brainpower than standard battle droids.

Droideka
Watch out! After rolling into battle, the droideka minifigure uncurls and destroys the enemy with its built-in blasters.

Buzz Droid
Buzz droids attack aircraft in swarms. They attach to starfighters and destroy them with their powerful circular saws.

Commander Droid
These minifigures are used on special missions because they are fast and very strong. They can withstand shots from most blasters.

MagnaGuard
This menacing minifigure is the bodyguard of General Grievous. He carries an electrostaff that even lightsabers can't break.

Luke Skywalker

Luke Skywalker appears in over 30 sets—more than any other minifigure in the LEGO *Star Wars* galaxy! His minifigures chart his incredible journey from a farmboy on Tatooine to a legendary pilot and Jedi hero. Which Luke minifigure do you like best?

Farmboy Luke
Young Luke meets Obi-Wan Kenobi and his life changes forever. He holds the lightsaber that once belonged to his father.

Stormtrooper Luke
Luke's minifigure wears stolen stormtrooper armor to sneak past real stormtroopers— the soldiers of the Imperial Army.

Celebration Luke
Luke's minifigure looks proud as he is awarded a medal for destroying the first Death Star.

Hoth Luke
Luke is on the ice planet Hoth at the Rebel base. His minifigure wears an extra-warm uniform and helmet. Brrr!

Pilot Luke
Luke becomes a pilot for the Rebel Alliance. Wearing an orange flightsuit, his X-wing pilot minifigure zooms into battle!

Infirmary Luke

After a deadly encounter with the wampa, Luke's minifigure wears an oxygen mask and straps to attach him to a healing bacta tank.

Trainee Jedi Luke

Luke is trained by Yoda. His minifigure works hard to build up strength—he even carries his Master!

Cloud City Luke

Luke's minifigure duels Darth Vader in the Cloud City set. His poor minifigure loses his right hand!

Jedi Luke

Luke is now a brave Jedi Knight. His minifigure has a black cybernetic hand and a new green lightsaber.

Endor Luke

Oh no! Imperial scout troopers are chasing Luke! But he is hard to spot, wearing a camouflage tunic.

Leia and Han

There are 11 minifigures of brave Rebel leader Princess Leia and 15 minifigures of Han Solo, the loveable rogue and unlikely hero of the Rebellion. Their minifigures showcase their many adventures as they fight to defeat the Empire. Which is your favorite?

Han Solo
This scruffy-looking minifigure is the confident pilot of the *Millennium Falcon*. His ship may look beaten-up, but it's fast.

Senator Leia
Senator Leia Organa is a secret supporter of the Rebel Alliance. Carrying a blaster, Leia's tough minifigure is not afraid to fight!

Stormtrooper Han
Han is disguised in stolen stormtrooper armor, but there is no mistaking his minifigure's trademark smile!

Hoth Han

He may be smiling, but Han hates the cold. It's a good thing his minifigure has a big hood!

Celebration Leia

Leia celebrates the destruction of the Death Star, but, look—she is always armed and ready!

Cloud City Leia

Leia's minifigure looks relaxed in casual clothes on Cloud City. But it's not long before she is caught in Darth Vader's trap!

Carbonite Han

Poor LEGO *Star Wars* Han has been frozen in a block of Carbonite! He is delivered to the evil crime lord Jabba the Hutt.

Slave Leia

Imprisoned by Jabba the Hutt, Leia is forced to wear a slave girl outfit and chain around her neck. Which minifigure will come to her rescue?

The Rebel Alliance

The Rebel Alliance is a brave group of minifigures who come together to fight the Imperial Army. They stand alongside Luke Skywalker, Princess Leia, and Han Solo, and their trusty companions, C-3PO, R2-D2, and Chewbacca, to defeat the Empire once and for all. Who is your favorite?

Mon Mothma
Mon Mothma leads the Rebel Alliance. She plans the Empire's downfall on board the LEGO *Star Wars* Rebel ship *Home One*.

Admiral Ackbar
This smartly dressed Mon Calamari minifigure is the clever commander of the Rebel Alliance's Navy.

General Lando Calrissian
Confident Lando is a Rebel general. With Ackbar, his minifigure launches a brave attack on the second Death Star.

R2-D2
R2-D2 is a resourceful little droid. His head piece has a holoprojector that can transmit vital hologram messages across the galaxy.

C-3PO
This nervous protocol droid helps different species to communicate with each other. Look—you can see some of his minifigure's wires!

Chewbacca

Wookiee Chewie is a loyal friend and companion to Han Solo. His minifigure is specially molded so that he looks hairy!

Hoth Rebel Trooper

Dressed for the cold, this minifigure works at the secret Rebel headquarters on the ice planet Hoth.

Crix Madine

Crix Madine is an important general. The badge on his minifigure's chest shows his rank.

Rebel Trooper

Wearing a blaster helmet and carrying a blaster gun, this heroic minifigure is ready to fight for the Alliance!

Rebel Commando

Dressed all in green, this minifigure is well-hidden in the trees as he keeps watch for stormtroopers on Endor.

Droid Power

The LEGO *Star Wars* galaxy is full of mechanical helpers that assist with all kinds of tasks. Some droid minifigures perform simple jobs, while others have more important tasks. But be careful—some are used for far more sinister purposes! Which droid minifigure would you like as your helper?

Mouse Droid

This minifigure is small and fast. It is perfect for delivering secret messages for the Empire without anyone noticing.

Treadwell Droid

This repair droid uses its four arm pieces to fix equipment. Each of its arms performs a different task.

FX-6

This medical droid has five arms, which prove very useful in operations. He brings Darth Vader back from the brink of death.

2-1B

2-1B is an intelligent surgical droid. His minifigure uses slow, precise movements to save Luke Skywalker.

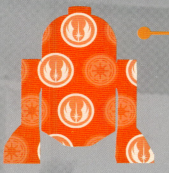

R2-Q5

In the LEGO *Star Wars* galaxy, you never know who is watching you! This droid uses his radar eye to spy for the Empire.

IT-O

The terrifying IT-O droid minifigure is used by the Empire to interrogate prisoners.

EV-9D9

Scary EV-9D9 works in Jabba's Palace. She loves to make other droids suffer, so it is a good thing she appears in just one LEGO set.

R-3PO

R-3PO works for the Rebel Alliance to catch Imperial spy droids. Bright red and moody, nobody would guess he is a spy detector!

R2-Q2

This astromech droid is used by Imperial forces. His minifigure stores the data for a huge map of the LEGO *Star Wars* galaxy.

Probe Droid

The Empire sends out these droids to find enemies. Its sensor eyes light up when it detects something. Look—one has lit up!

R5-D8

Astromech droids can repair starships and co-pilot them too. This droid co-pilots an X-wing in the attack on the Death Star.

The Imperial Army

The Empire has one of the most powerful armies in LEGO *Star Wars* history. These military minifigures rule through fear and violence. They are trained to invade planets across the galaxy—and they plan to crush the Rebellion! Which LEGO minifigure looks the scariest to you?

Stormtrooper
Stormtroopers are fiercely loyal to the Empire. These faceless minifigures wear identical white armor and carry blasters.

Sandtrooper
This minifigure is covered in sand—he has been searching for C-3P0 and R2-D2 on the desert planet Tatooine.

Snowtrooper
Snowtroopers wear heated suits and helmets with built-in snow goggles for exploring ice planets.

Scout Trooper
Scout troopers are sent out on very dangerous missions. They wear helmets with visors for spotting the enemy.

AT-AT Driver
These minifigures drive deadly AT-AT walkers. They wear special equipment to allow them to breathe on different planets.

AT-ST Driver
This minifigure pilots the All Terrain Scout Transport. He takes his job very seriously and is prepared for battle with a blaster and anti-shock helmet.

Royal Guard
This mysterious-looking minifigure is Emperor Palpatine's personal bodyguard. He is a deadly warrior!

Grand Moff Tarkin
Grand Moff Tarkin is one of the most powerful and feared officer minifigures in the Empire.

Imperial Officer
This minifigure does not need to carry any weapons because he works far away from the battlefields on the Imperial shuttle.

Death Star Trooper
This scowling minifigure is part of a specially trained fighting force aboard the Death Star.

Space Pilots

These minifigures are among the greatest pilots in the LEGO *Star Wars* galaxy. They all have good reflexes, strong nerve, lots of confidence, and awesome—or in some cases, fearsome—reputations. But who do you think is the best pilot minifigure in the galaxy?

A-Wing Pilot
A-wing pilots fly the fastest starfighters in the galaxy! These minifigures are part of the Rebel Alliance's Green Squadron.

B-Wing Pilot
Wearing a red jumpsuit, this Rebel minifigure pilots the largest single-seat starship in the galaxy.

Ten Numb
This pilot leads a Rebel attack in the Battle of Endor. The Sullustan minifigure has large eyes and a creased face.

Jek Porkins
Jek is a brave pilot, who flies his X-wing in the attack on the first Death Star. His minifigure is given the nickname Piggy.

Zev Senesca
A daring minifigure, Zev flies his Rebel X-wing on Hoth. He always makes sure that he keeps his blaster close to hand!

Skyhopper Pilot

This ace pilot races his friends on Tatooine. Could this mysterious minifigure be Luke Skywalker under the helmet and goggles?

Naboo Pilot

Naboo has been invaded! This fighter pilot minifigure must defend his home planet in his N-1 starfighter.

TIE Fighter Pilot

This minifigure is an elite pilot of the Imperial Navy. Rebels call these pilots "bucketheads" due to their bulky helmets.

Gold Leader

Y-wing and X-wing pilot minifigures wear life-support units to help them breathe in space.

Juno Eclipse

Juno Eclipse is on a top-secret mission! Her minifigure has to fly Darth Vader's secret apprentice across the galaxy.

On the Hunt

Watch out! These minifigures are the most-feared bounty hunters in the LEGO *Star Wars* galaxy. They are hired to track down wanted minifigures for credits. They come from different planets and backgrounds, but they are all scary! Which minifigure would you least like on your trail?

Aurra Sing
Aurra Sing once trained to be a Jedi, but she is now a ruthless bounty hunter. Her minifigure carries two pistols.

Bossk
Look at this bounty hunter's terrifying teeth! Han Solo and Chewbacca better watch out—he has a grudge against them.

Embo
Embo is a Kyuzo bounty hunter. He carries a bowcaster, but he has another secret weapon— his metal hat!

Dengar
Dangerous Dengar always carries a huge blaster rifle. His minifigure wears pieces of battered stormtrooper armor.

Cad Bane
This villainous minifigure uses his twin blasters to attack the Jedi. He is a Duros with blue skin and scary red eyes.

Jango Fett

This legendary bounty hunter swoops into action using his jetpack. Carrying custom-made blasters, he is ready to attack!

Shahan Alama

This minifigure was kicked out of his pirate gang for being too mean! He now works with fellow bounty hunter Cad Bane.

Greedo

This Rodian bounty hunter has been hired to search for Han Solo. But, strangely, his minifigure is unarmed!

Boba Fett

Boba Fett is a great bounty hunter like his father Jango. His helmet has a rangefinder for tracking down his targets.

Sugi

Sugi is a deadly Zabrak bounty hunter. Her minifigure carries a blaster and a lethal vibroblade.

Jabba's Palace

Jabba the Hutt is an enormous slug-like crime lord who conducts shady dealings across the LEGO *Star Wars* galaxy. Jabba's desert palace is brought to life through the strange minifigures that inhabit it. Which minifigure do you think is the creepiest?

Jabba the Hutt
This slimy, green gangster has a huge appetite! Jabba's supersized minifigure is made up of one large LEGO piece and two tail pieces.

Bib Fortuna
Bib Fortuna is Jabba's assistant. This eerie minifigure decides who can talk to Jabba.

B'omarr Monk
These strange minifigures contain the live brains of the original owners of the palace. The brains are carried around on droid legs.

Gamorrean Guard
This Gamorrean is strong, but stupid—so he does whatever Jabba tells him to! He stands guard with a deadly vibroax.

Rotta the Hutt
Rotta is green and slimy, like his father. But unlike Jabba, his minifigure is tiny!

The Jedi

Rebel Trooper

Geonosian Zombie

Cody

Commander Gree

Captain Rex

Rebel Commando

Juno Eclipse

Biggs Darklighter

Thi-Sen

Saesee Tiin

Endor Luke

R5-J2

Commander Fox

Yoda

©2012 LEGO

Clone Troopers

Zev Senesca

©2012 LEGO

General Lando Calrissian

©2012 LEGO

Qui-Gon Jinn

©2012 LEGO

C-3PO

©2012 LEGO

Gungan

©2012 LEGO

Count Dooku's Pilot Droid

©2012 LEGO

Quinlan Vos

©2012 LEGO

Ten Numb

©2012 LEGO

B-Wing Pilot

©2012 LEGO

Padmé

©2012 LEGO

Wookiee Warrior

©2012 LEGO

Mace Windu

©2012 LEGO

Luminara Unduli

©2012 LEGO

Bomb Squad Trooper

Han Solo

Ahsoka and Rotta

Senator Leia

Admiral Ackbar

Embo

Ben Kenobi

Farmboy Luke

Commander Cody

Mon Mothma

Ahsoka Tano

Kashyyyk Trooper

Ki-Adi-Mundi

Hoth Rebel Trooper

©2012 LEGO

Black
Ewok

Wampa Cave
Skeleton

Crix
Madine

Jar Jar Binks

Obi-Wan
Kenobi

Celebration
Leia

Chewbacca

Lobot

Jedi
Luke

Chief
Chirpa

Jedi
Knight

Hoth
Luke

Hoth
Leia

R2-D2

©2012 LEGO

Star Corps
Trooper

Stormtrooper
Luke

Clone
Pilot

A-Wing
Pilot

Trainee
Jedi
Luke

Brave
Obi-Wan

Watto

ARC
Trooper

Celebration
Luke

Hondo
Ohnaka

Aerial
Trooper

Gungan
Soldier

Barriss
Offee

Shaak Ti

©2012 LEGO

Slave
Leia

Pilot
Luke

Clone
Trooper

Lando in
Disguise

©2012 LEGO

Jedi
Lightsabers

K-3PO

Commander
Wolffe

Assassin
Droid

©2012 LEGO

Cloud
City
Luke

Onaconda
Farr

Shock
Trooper

Aayla Secura

Logray

Obi-Wan
"Ben"
Kenobi

Stormtrooper Han

IG-88

Eeth Koth

Imperial Shuttle Pilot

Captain Panaka

Hoth Han

Lightsaber duel

©2012 LEGO

Naboo Pilot

Carbonite Han

Infirmary Luke

Clone Commando Captain

Jek Porkins

Plo Koon

General Grievous

Nahdar Vebb

Wicket W. Warrick

Cloud City Leia

Wald

GNK Droid

Pit Droid

Jango Fett

TIE Fighter Pilot

Gold Leader

Tusken Raider

Zam Wesell

Paploo

Jawa

Battle Droid

Parka Anakin

IT-O

Probe Droid

Injured Anakin

Greedo

Droid Commander

FX-6

Sentry Droid

©2012 LEGO

Skyhopper Pilot

R2-Q5

Celebration Han

Kit Fisto

Parka Han

Treadwell Droid

Jedi Anakin

Chancellor Palpatine

Commander Droid

Security Battle Droid

R-3PO

Young Boba Fett

2-1B

Clone Wars Anakin

Meet Darth Vader

Super Battle Droid

©2012 LEGO

Gamorrean Guard

Geonosian Battle Droid

B'omarr Monk

Aurra Sing

Droideka

A4-D

Buzz Droid

Podracer Anakin

Darth Maul

Turk Falso

Darth Vader

Asajj Ventress

Security Battle Droid

EV-9D9

©2012 LEGO

Brave
Qui-Gon
Jinn

Boy
Anakin

©2012 LEGO

Death Star
Trooper

©2012 LEGO

Nute
Gunray

©2012 LEGO

Death
Star
Droid

©2012 LEGO

Sebulba

©2012 LEGO

Royal Guard

©2012 LEGO

Count
Dooku

©2012 LEGO

Savage
Opress

©2012 LEGO

Rocket Droid
Commander

©2012 LEGO

R1-G4

©2012 LEGO

Emperor
Palpatine

R2-Q2

Padawan Anakin

©2012 LEGO

©2012 LEGO

©2012 LEGO

General
Veers

©2012 LEGO

R5-D8

Mouse
Droid

Grand Moff
Tarkin

Mandalorian

AT-AT
Driver

Bossk

Recon
Trooper

Sugi

General
Grievous

Hologram
Palpatine

Battle-Damaged Anakin

Sith Apprentice
Anakin

Owen Lars

Scout
Trooper

©2012 LEGO

Cad Bane

Shadow Trooper

Jabba the Hutt

Rotta the Hutt

Imperial Officer

Shahan Alama

Dengar

Stormtrooper

Clone Commander

Bib Fortuna

Heroic Han

Galen Marek

Endor Leia

Gasgano

©2012 LEGO

Siege
Battalion
Trooper

Snowtrooper

Sandtrooper

AT-ST
Driver

Embo

X-Wing
Pilot

Aldar
Beedo

Boba Fett

Clone
Gunner

Geonosian
Warrior

Clone
Pilot

Darth
Maul

Wampa

MagnaGuard

©2012 LEGO